THE ANGEL IN HIS LIFE
VIBERT MILLER

This book is a work of fiction. All names of characters and all incidents are products of the author's imagination. Any resemblance to persons, living or dead, is entirely coincidental.

Cover design by V. A. Miller

CHAPTER ONE

Joseph Sommers was awakened from a sound sleep by someone shaking him by his shoulder. He raised up to find a very beautiful woman looking down at him. He didn't know who she was, he had never seen her before but here she was in his bedroom, standing over him.

"Who are you?" he said, "and how the hell did you get in here? I'm sure I locked my door last night."

"Don't talk to me about hell," she said, "my name is Bethany and I didn't use your door."

"Well how the he.. sorry, how did you get in?" he said. "You climbed through a window? I'm eight stories up."

"Do I look like someone who would climb through a window?"

"No. Okay did Tony send you. He likes to play jokes like this."

"I don't know a Tony. Oh, yes I do. But he died about three hundred years ago."

"Hold on," he said, "I don't like where this conversation is going. Why are you here?"

"I came to deliver a message."

"What message?"

"The message is you should stop messing around and finish your novel."

"If you know about my novel then you should know I didn't finish it because I have writer's block."

"What is that? I think you're just being lazy. Buck up, put pen to paper and finish it."

"For your information writers don't put pen to paper anymore. We use computers."

"Okay, put pen to computer and finish it. I'll be back later to check on you."

She started toward his bedroom door and walked right through it without opening it. If Tony was behind this, he knew things Joe didn't. He slapped his face hard just to convince himself he didn't dream what just happened. He walked into the small room he used as an office and his computer was on the desk where he left it with the unfinished novel. Bethany claimed she knew nothing about writer's block. If she could walk through walls she should know about writer's block, And what was that about knowing a Tony but he's been dead for about three hundred years. That was one hell of a dream. Tony would get a kick out of this. He called him and asked him to meet for lunch.

Anthony Ward was Joe's good friend and agent. He was good at his job and was responsible for seeing his books land at good publishers. He was continually pushing Joe to complete whatever he was writing and he could say he owed a lot of his success to him. But this time he outdid himself.

They greeted each when he arrived at the restaurant where Tony had already secured a table.

"Your messenger came last night," Joe told him, "I don't know how you and she pulled that off but it was effective."

"What are you talking about?" Tony asked, "what messenger?"

"Oh, come on Tony," he said, "Beth. She came last night although I have no idea how she got into my apartment."

"Have you been drinking, Joe," he said, "because I have no idea what you're going on about."

"You didn't send Bethany?"

"I don't even know anyone by the name of Bethany," he said.

He told him about what he thought was his dream. Tony was looking at him so closely it made him uncomfortable.

"Joseph Sommers," he said, "I think that fertile imagination of yours has run amok. I expect to see all of this in a future novel. In the meantime, why are you dragging your feet on the one you're writing. Your deadline is almost upon us. I think your Bethany is spot on, you're using writer's block as an excuse."

"She's not *my* Bethany. I've never seen the woman before. But maybe she has a point. Maybe I've been dragging my feet. Are you sure you didn't set me up?"

"With a woman who walks through walls? Hardly."

He left Tony with a promise to buckle down and finish the novel and when he walked into his office Bethany was standing over his computer, reading.

"Hey, I found out about computers," she said, "and I've been reading what you've written. Not bad. You have a real flair for words."

"Bethany," he said, "we need to have a serious talk. Who are you, really?"

"For a prize-winning author you're not too bright. Haven't you figured out that I'm an angel?"

"An angel?"

"Yes. And we are concerned about you."

"Who is 'we'? he asked.

"A bunch of angels. We drew straws as to who should come talk to you. I drew the short one."

"So, what is your job, exactly?"

"My job, exactly, is to push you to stop being so lazy."

"I'm not being lazy. I have writer's block."

"There's that word again. I'm going to find out what that is. If you're not lying to me I may be able to help you."

Bethany did not stop by for the next week but she must have found out about writer's block and did something, because suddenly he was hit with a spurt of intense inspiration and the words just tumbled out of his brain. Tony was impressed with how much he had accomplished.

"I think you're going to make your deadline with time to spare. What happened?"

"I don't know," he said, "but suddenly I broke through my block and I'm seeing the end." He wasn't about to tell him he thought Bethany had something to do with it.

The book was finished and he celebrated by dozing off in his armchair only to be awakened by Bethany.

"I wish you wouldn't sneak up on me," he said.

"Sorry about that," she said, "I see you're finished. Congratulations."

"Thanks to you," he said.

"Don't thank me," she said, "I had nothing to do with it. It was all your doing. You should be proud of yourself."

"I guess your job is done so I won't see you again," Joe said."

"No. I will be around for a while. You're starting another book, right?"

He admitted he was glad to hear that. He had grown accustomed to having her around and didn't want to say goodbye. She said she didn't but he was sure she had something to do with the disappearance of his writer's block. Could angels lie? He knew almost nothing about angels and their existence. He always thought they only were present in fairy tales for children. But here he was, an adult and a writer of some repute communing with an angel. If this got out, the gentlemen with the white coats wouldn't be far behind. He received word from Tony that the publishers liked his book and had already put it in their schedule. This called for a celebration and Tony was buying. They were sitting at the bar of their favorite place when his arm was jostled by a woman trying to retrieve her drink from the barman. She apologized but there was no harm done. Joe told her so but she insisted on buying his next round. She also told him she was sitting alone at a table for two and would be pleased if he would join her. He looked at Tony who waved him off to go ahead and join her.

She told him her name was Madelyn Sawyer and she was an attorney in her own practice. She asked what he did for a living and when he said he was a writer she said, "like a correspondent for a newspaper or magazine?"

"No, I write fiction," he said.

"Oh, I have to admit I recently launched my own practice," she said, "and since I'm the only lawyer on the premises, my nose is always buried in law books." She did not know who Joseph Sommers was and that suited him. Tony caught his eye and signaled he wanted to talk to him. He shook his head okay. He came over to where Joe was sitting and said, "can I have a quick word?" Joe introduced him to Madelyn and after shaking his hand she said, "you guys talk. I have to go to the ladies room."

"I may have to skip out on you," Tony said, "I hope you don't mind."

Joe looked over to the stool he was occupying and there was a lady on it. "Don't mind, my friend," he said, "good luck."

Madelyn made her way back from the ladies room and stood by his chair.

"Do you mind if I call it a night," she said, "I'm really beat. Very long day." She fumbled in her purse and came up with a business card on the back of which she jotted down her personal number and handed it to him. He didn't have card so he wrote his number on a napkin and handed it to her.

"I'm going to say goodnight," she said, "call me?"

He picked up his glass and raised it to her, "shall I say it?" he said.

"You shall," she said.

And he said it, "here's looking at you kid."

CHAPTER TWO

When Joe went through his pockets the next morning he came upon Madelyn's card and put her personal number into his phone. He had planned to fix a substantial breakfast but decided, instead, to go out. He called Tony and invited him to breakfast. The first thing he asked Joe was, if he was paying. When Joe told him he would, after calling him a cheapskate, Tony accepted. He asked Tony how things went with his date. He said it was fine but he didn't think he would see her again because she was quite the talker. He was sure he would not ask her out. Then he asked if Joe intended to see his lady again.

"Madelyn? Right?" he said, "she looked fine."

"Yes. I will probably ask her out," Joe said, "she gave me her number before I asked for it."

They lingered over breakfast with three cups of coffee each, then shook hands on the sidewalk and took separate taxis home. Later that day he was making good on his promise to call Madelyn when he looked up and was staring at Bethany.

"What?" he said.

"What do you mean?" Madelyn asked.

"Sorry, Madelyn," he said, "I have to call you back," and ended the call.

"What are you doing here?" he asked Bethany, "are you stalking me?"

"Stalking? No, never."

"Then why are you here in my apartment?"

"I'm supposed to make sure you're okay. You haven't started your new book yet."

"You've invaded my privacy," he said, "I need to talk to your boss."

"My boss? Oh, you mean Mickey," she said, and became anxious. She clearly didn't want him to talk to this Mickey, whom he took to be the angel who was over all of them.

She explained it would mean trouble for her since she was on probation because of a mess she made of a previous assignment. Her job in that assignment, was to steer a wealthy man from an ill-advised investment but she became distracted and the man made the investment and lost all his money. They put the blame squarely on her shoulders and put her on probation. Joe was her chance to redeem herself and that was why she was constantly in his face.

"I'm sorry about what happened," he said, "but I can't allow you to invade my life."

"That woman you're calling won't be good for you," she said.

"How do you know who I was calling?" he said, "don't bother to answer that. You probably were there but were invisible."

"I was visible but I was sitting at the end of the bar. You won't believe how many men tried to hit on me."

"Of course, they did," he said, "you're a beautiful woman."

"You think I'm beautiful?" she said.

"Have you looked in a mirror lately?"

"It doesn't do any good. When an angel is on probation nothing appears in a mirror. That's how we know if we're off probation. The mirror shows our reflection."

"Well, you can take my word. You're beautiful."

"Are you trying to hit on me?"

"What would you do if I am?"

"Nothing. Angels and humans can't get together," she said. And then added, "what's the new book about?"

He hadn't thought about that and was about to say so when an idea struck him. "It's about a Guardian Angel who intervenes in a man's life and causes him nothing but grief."

She didn't miss a beat, "then it will be a best seller," she said, "because that's what's happening to you." He was about to reply to that but she was gone. He decided to call Madelyn later.

Tony called to ask if he had started his new novel. He told him not yet but he had the idea for the book. He told him what he had told Beth and he could sense his hesitation.

"Joe," he said, "your readers expect a thriller from you. Now you're talking about angels? What the hell do you know about angels anyway?"

He did not tell him he knew a lot about angels since one was practically living in his apartment and she was quite something.

He called Madelyn the next day and was met with a barrage of fury. She wanted to know why he did not call her back as soon as possible. he was blindsided by her attitude. He was calling to ask if she wanted to have dinner with him but the whole idea was now repulsive to him. He apologized for bothering her and ended the call. It occurred to him Bethany was right on when she said Madelyn was not for him. He debated whether or not he should admit this to Bethany. But she probably already knew.

His problem was how to incorporate an angel into the thriller he was going to write. His thrillers were the usual good guys against bad guys so, he was thinking good angels against bad angels and were there such things as bad angels. He made a note to ask Bethany the next time she came by.

"I have no idea," she said, when he posed the question to her. "But I don't think so. If there are bad entities they won't be called angels."

This was of no help to him and he told her so. "Sorry," she said, "I haven't been an angel very long."

"How long?" he asked.

"Only about a three hundred years. Some angels go back a thousand years."

He wanted to know more about Bethany. He wanted to know how she died. Did she die peacefully or violently.

"Die?" she asked. "Joe, I am not a ghost. Nobody died for me to be an angel. I think you are confusing angels and ghosts."

"So, angels are just created to be the helpmeet of humans," he said. "and you must follow the rules."

"And one of those rules is that angels and humans can't get together in a romantic sense."

"I'm asking for my book," he said. "Can you tell me about how you were created?"

"Oh, no I don't know how that happened. I only know I was talking to Mickey and he was telling me about my first assignment. Mickey is the one who hands out assignments."

"Okay, one more question. Do angels gather somewhere?"

"No, we're spread out among the stars."

He wanted to question her more but she disappeared without saying goodbye. He resolved to let her know the next time she came to him, he would like her to tell him she was leaving and not just abruptly disappear. He started writing his new book and immediately got bogged down with how to introduce his angel character to his readers. He always wanted to tell a story in which the strong lead character was female and he would do that in this book. To give her even more power she would be guided by a male angel. He reached that point then went blank. He was sure Bethany would accuse him of being lazy if he used the writer's block excuse so he decided to keep that out of the conversation. But he failed to recognize she could see through him.

"Don't tell me you're using that writer's block again," she said.

"Do you know what writer's block is?" he said.

"Sure. Its another word for lazy," she replied.

"Obviously you don't know much about writing," he said.

"No, but I know many writers and I've never heard them moan about writer's block."

"I should have a word with your boss," he said, "and tell him you're not nice to me."

"Ha, you do that and he's liable to send someone who is tougher than I am. I'm a softie compared to some other angels."

"Also, I wish you wouldn't just disappear," he said, "it would be nice if you said goodbye when you leave."

"Touchy, aren't we," she said, "okay I can do that and right now. Bye."

With that last word he was left alone in his apartment, to wonder if she would weave her magic and help him get over his block.

Two weeks later he was still bogged down and she had not returned. He wondered if he had seen the last of her and that thought gave him pause.

CHAPTER THREE

Joe was sitting on his sofa watching a football game when he felt her presence and she materialized.

"Did you miss me?" she asked. "I last saw you three weeks ago."

"I thought you were in the background being invisible."

"Nope. I stayed away so you could get on with your book, but I see there hasn't been much progress."

"Do you have substance?" he asked out of the blue.

"What do you mean?"

"What would happen if I touched you?"

"Are you getting fresh with me? Of course, I have substance. Here, take my hand."

He took her hand and it was soft and warm, as it should be.

"Why did you think I had no substance?" she said

"I saw you walk through a wall," he said, "I can't do that."

"How do you know you can't? You ever tried it?"

"No. I just know I can't."

"Follow me," she said and walked toward the wall. Without effort she disappeared through it. He followed and his nose impacted the wall. He didn't break it but came close. She appeared on his side of the wall giggling when she saw him rubbing my nose.

"You told me to follow you," he said in embarrassment.

"Yeah but I didn't think you would be foolish enough to do it." This was the first time he saw this side of Bethany. She was a jokester. She asked how his book was coming and when he told her he was considering abandoning the project because his knowledge of angels was zero, she reminded him he had personal acquaintance with one.

"Don't spread that around," he said. "Do you know what people would think if they knew I talk to an angel?"

"That you're a lucky man?"

"No. That I have a loose screw,"

Joe received an invitation to a charity ball to raise funds for an organization devoted to helping needy children. He was a constant supporter of the organization so he was invited. Bethany materialized in his living room as he was reading the invitation.

"I guess that is from your publisher scolding you for being lazy," she said.

"No. It is an invitation to a ball. But I don't plan to attend. Here, read it," he gave it to her.

"Why not attend?" she said, "it sounds like a big deal."

"It is a big deal. But mostly couples will be there. I will stick out, flying solo."

"You can take me," she said.

"What? I can't take you. You're an angel."

"Only you will know that. And I'm sure you won't tell."

"It's black tie," he said, "that means formal wear. Do you have formal wear?"

"I know what black tie means," she said, "I can get formal wear. I'm an angel, remember?"

He leased a limousine and driver for the evening. He told Bethany what time she should be at his place and she arrived at the exact time. She looked like she had just stepped off the pages of a high fashion magazine, resplendent in a blue gown, her hair curled up on her head and a diamond necklace around her neck. He stared at her and all he could get out was "wow."

"Do you approve?" she said.

"Definitely," he said, "where did you..."

"Later," she said, "the car is waiting."

Bethany turned heads. He was the envy of every man in the room all wondering when did he get so lucky. He noticed she liked champagne and was drinking it down too fast but when he mentioned that to her she told him it was okay, angels could not get drunk. She was wrong. When she began to slur her words, he decided it was time for them to leave. He wasn't sure what to do with a drunk angel so he just got her into the limo and they headed home. She fell asleep in the car and he had to wake her when they arrived at his apartment. She held on to him as they rode up in the elevator and collapsed on the sofa when he got her into the apartment.

"You can sleep it off in the guest room," he said and took her to the door. "There is a nightgown in the closet. You can put it on."

"You have a nightgown in your closet?"

"Yes. It belongs to a woman I used to date but we broke up and she never claimed her nightgown."

"If she had a nightgown here, it means you were more than just dating," she said. He didn't answer. He just closed the door and left her alone. He expected her to disappear during the night but he was wrong. He was sitting at his kitchen counter when she appeared dressed in the nightgown. He had the television on to watch the morning news, when a reporter of local news came on to say a high end fashion store reported they were robbed of a very expensive gown. Their surprise was that nothing else was taken and they could not understand it. At the same time a jewelry store reported they were robbed of a very expensive diamond necklace. Bethany saw the news at the same time and left the room.

"You have anything to do with those robberies?" he said, "that picture of the gown looks exactly like the one you were wearing. You stole them?"

"Angels don't steal," she said. "We sometimes borrow stuff. I intended to return them before the stores opened this morning but you got me drunk last night and I slept late."

"I didn't get you drunk. You didn't know when to stop guzzling the champagne. You told me angels couldn't get drunk."

"I was wrong," she said, "I will return them after the stores close tonight. I didn't embarrass you did I?"

"No. I got you out of there before you got to that point. You looked great. That gown was made for you and that necklace sparkled so much it almost blinded me. Are you going to get into trouble for being drunk?"

"I don't know. I don't think it has ever happened before."

"Well, drunk or not you were a perfect lady. And I can bear witness to that." She held her head as is if she were listening.

"I have to go," She said gathering up the gown and necklace and disappearing into the guest room. He waited about five minutes before knocking on the door. He could not hear anything coming from the room so he opened the door and entered. The room was empty. The gown and necklace were gone and so was the nightgown he loaned her. She left in the nightgown but he knew she would return it the next time she visited.

He suddenly felt fear that she would not be allowed to return because she got drunk on his watch. He wished there was some way he could have a talk with this man she called Mickey who was her handler.

Mickey came to see him. He was watching a movie on television when his door opened and he came in.

"I'm sure I locked that door," he said. "How did you get in?"

"It was locked," he said, "but we have our ways."

"Hold on," he said, "you must be Mickey."

"Very good, Mr. Sommers," Mickey said, "then you must know why I'm here."

"Yeah. You're here because Bethany had a little too much champagne. If you expect me to say anything bad about her, you've wasted your time."

"I was thinking of assigning another angel to you if..."

"Stop right there. I don't want another angel. If you think I need an angel in my life, it has to be Bethany. I will not accept any other. I have a say in this don't I?"

"Yes, you do. Can you tell me why you insist on Bethany?"

"Sure. She's tough and don't let me slack off but she's also fun with a great sense of humor. I like that."

"Okay, Mr. Sommers," Mickey said getting to his feet, "Bethany will return." This time he didn't bother to open the door, he just walked through it.

There was a story running on the television about the return of the pricey gown and the diamond necklace. When the stores opened for business the next morning the items were back in place. They concluded the items were not stolen, just borrowed. What lent credence to the story was a woman said she was at a gala and was sure she saw a woman wearing the gown. Another woman said she too was at the gala and saw the necklace and thought the wearer must be very wealthy because those were all diamonds. But they could not provide police with a description of the wearer. The story soon faded from the news since no harm was done.

Two weeks later Bethany stopped by. She was all smiles when she saw Joe. "Mickey told me what you said," she said, "thank you."

"Anything to help my favorite angel," he said, "so, you're off the hook?"

"Yes and remind me not to ever drink champagne again."

"Your problem was you drank too much of it," he said. "thinking it could not affect you."

CHAPTER FOUR

Joe told Tony he was seriously considering dropping his current project and starting up something new. Tony was against the idea. He told him he had already mentioned the story idea involving an angel to the publishers and they were very enthusiastic. They thought it would bring in a whole new group of readers. To them it meant people who were not thrilled about thrillers might be, if an angel was involved. He urged Joe to continue but was dismayed when Joe told him he had not yet written one word of the book.

"You need to get your butt in gear," Tony said, "they're expecting a manuscript in six months."

Joe met Ann Sampson through a dating site. He was not interested in getting a date but he wanted some firsthand knowledge about the workings of a dating site for the story he was working on. As soon as his fake credentials went live he received a hit from Ann Sampson. She said she was three years younger than he was but her picture showed a pretty woman about ten years his junior. This alerted him to be cautious but he assumed she was trying to be just as cautious as he was. There was no harm in corresponding with a good looking woman. They texted back and forth for a couple weeks until she surprised him by telling him they should meet. This not only surprised him but had consequences for his character who, like him, was under the impression only the man initiated the meet up scenario and the woman always was reluctant. But here the woman was asking to meet. So far they had not exchanged names. Her handle was Teach 101 and his was Writer Block. He agreed to meet with her, drawing skepticism from Bethany. She wanted to accompany him under the cloak of invisibility. he flatly turned that down.

"I don't want you looking over my shoulder," he said. "You have to stay away. I have no way of knowing if you're with me so I have to rely on your promise. Cross your heart and hope to...oh damn, that doesn't mean anything. Raise your right hand."

"Please, Joe," she pleaded, "I just want to be sure you're not making a mistake. Remember that other woman? I promise, you won't know I'm there. I don't like the way she initiated meeting with you."

He, too, thought that was strange. "Okay you can come. But I don't want to know you're around.'"

He met Ann in a restaurant on the edge of town. She was dressed in an outfit that screamed sexy and he immediately regretted not dressing up for the occasion. He apologized and she set his mind at ease by telling him it's normal for guys not to dress up for a first meeting whereas girls always want to make a good first impression. Hell, he thought, a man should also want to make a good first impression too, but he didn't belabor the point. He ordered a bottle of white wine to get them started. They raised their glasses to toast their meeting but somehow her glass never made it to her mouth and she poured wine all over her blouse. She jumped back and started apologizing for her carelessness.

"Go to bathroom quickly," he said, "and use towels to dry off. Fortunately, it is not red wine. That would have stained more. White wine will come out in the wash, red won't."

As soon as she left there was whispering in his ear. He knew it was Bethany.

"You promised," he said, holding up the menu to cover his lips.

"Sorry. I had to intervene. She is a guy."

"What? What guy?" he said. getting a little upset.

"Your friend is a man."

"A man? How do you know this? She looks like a very pretty woman to me."

"She is a man. I looked."

"What do you mean you looked? Can you see through clothes?"

"Yes. I can. That woman is a man."

He was staring at a point where he thought she was standing. "Can you see through my clothes?"

"Yes. But I've never looked. Here she comes back. Be cool."

The wine had run down on to the front of the designer slacks she was wearing an everything was revealed.

"Wow," he said, "you seem to be well endowed."

"What?" she looked down to where Joe was looking. "Oh my God ," she said and ran out of the restaurant.

He put the menu before his face and was pretending to study it. "You might as well sit with me," he whispered. "Go back and come in as a person and pretend I'm a friend you just happen to see."

He saw her talking to the hostess and pointing in his direction. Then the hostess brought her over. He stood and they embraced like two friends who happened on each other.

"Okay," he said, after the hostess left, "you can say it. You saved me from a very embarrassing situation."

"It's nothing. That's what angels are for. Your embarrassment would have been greater the first time you ended up in bed with her."

"Please don't remind me. I can cancel our dinner if you'd prefer not to stay."

"Why waste a good meal." Bethany said, "let's stay and enjoy. I don't think you'll be hearing from Teach 101 again."

"Did you have anything to do with him spilling wine on himself?"

"I had to speak to you and I needed to get him away. The idiot couldn't find his mouth."

On the way home in a taxi she said, "goodbye, for now," and she was gone. She didn't bother to open the door of the taxi.

He had to rewrite the chapter in which his character's actions were based on his notion that only men initiated a meet up. Then he had to put it back because Teach 101 was a man after all, disguised as a woman.

He was not comfortable with the idea Bethany could see through his clothes. But then he thought if she wanted to sneak a peek, he didn't care, as long as he made sure to always wear clean underwear. His book gathered momentum and he decided to make his experience with Teach 101 a part of one chapter. Since his book was fiction he could use the experience in any way he wanted. His mistake was not giving his angel her due. She had his computer open to the scene in the restaurant where she rescued him and he could tell she was searching for her name, and didn't find it.

"Aren't you forgetting something?" she said.

"I don't think so," he replied, "what am I forgetting?"

"Who saved you from embarrassment?" she asked.

"You did but I didn't think you wanted me to mention you. Aren't you supposed to work incognito?"

"Who told you that? I don't want my name mentioned but you should be able to find some way to give credit where credit is due. You are supposed to be a bestselling author."

He knew now, this angel he stood up for against her boss, was expecting him to give her a place in his novel. She was turning everything he thought he knew about angels, on its head and he was not sure what to make of it. He rewrote the restaurant scene for the third time and found a way to give her credit without giving the impression he was socializing with an angel.

He encouraged her to read the restaurant experience again. She did and a broad smile broke out on her face.

"I knew you could do it," she said, "all you needed was a little prodding."

Bethany kept on prodding him all the way to the end of the novel, which he turned in long before it was due.

"This is a surprise," Tony said, "it's the first time you've completed a book ahead of schedule. What happened? Not that I'm complaining mind you."

"Nothing happened," he replied, "I just felt the inspiration and the words kept coming."

He thought he would probably catch hell from Bethany for not letting on she was the inspiration he talked about. But she said nothing on that subject.

His publishers declared it was his best work. They especially liked how he wove an angel into the story without diminishing the thriller aspect of it. It was still a story of good guys facing off against bad guys, but with an angel in the midst to elevate the story to a higher level. He didn't see it that way exactly because he groused every time Bethany prodded him, but if that would sell books, he was all for it. He received a large advance from the publishers and decided to take Bethany to dinner.

"You mean as a person?" she asked.

"Of course, as a person," he said, "if you're invisible it would appear I'm talking to myself and that wouldn't be good."

"How should I dress?" she said.

"Casual."

"Good. I know just where I can borrow a nice outfit."

CHAPTER FIVE

All through dinner he could tell Bethany was anxious to ask him something and she blurted it out during dessert.

"When are you starting on your next book?" she said.

"Hold on," he said, "I just finished a book. Don't I get some time off?"

"You deserve it," she said, "but here is the problem." She went on to detail the problem. She was assigned to him as his muse and if he were not writing, he did not need a muse so, she would be taken away from him. She didn't want that and neither did he. The only way he could keep her was by writing, so he started another project.

"What will the new book be about?" Bethany said.

"My last book with the angel was so well received," he said, "I'm following up with another story with an angel. But this time the angel will fall in love with her human."

"No, no, that can't happen. Angels cannot fall in love with humans. It is not allowed."

"I'm writing fiction. All things are possible," he said.

"True," she said, "but you cannot go against nature."

"Would it be against nature if I were to fall in love with you?" he asked her. He could see disbelief written all over her face.

"Are you?" she asked..

"I'm just posing a hypothetical question," he said.

"Oh, I see. I really don't know. All I've been told is that angels and humans are not supposed to mix."

"Is that against a law?"

"We don't have many laws but we do have rules and that is one of them."

It was one evening in early Spring, when the trees had shaken off their winter dullness and were putting out new buds, that his world collapsed around him. He spoke to his mother earlier that day while she was preparing to receive guests. It was her turn to host her card playing group and she was looking forward to it. He cautioned her to take it easy because she had a weak heart and wore a pace maker. She assured him she was fine. But she was not. When his phone rang, a dark cloud descended around him. He knew that call meant sadness. His mom had collapsed and was rushed to the hospital. One of her friends was on the phone to tell him the news.

Joe broke several speed laws to get to the hospital and was taken to the room where they were working on her. Her heart had stopped in the ambulance but the doctors had managed to get it beating again. Her private physician was called and he came out to talk to Joe. He was also Joe's doctor so he knew him well.

"I'm so sorry, Joe," he said, "she suffered a massive attack. We were able to restart her heart but I don't know how long she will last."

"Can I see her?" he asked.

"Of course. She asked for you. But don't stay too long. I don't want her to exert herself talking."

His mother was a small woman but she looked even smaller lying in that hospital bed. She looked like a child. Her face lit up when she saw Joe and she tried to squeeze his hand when he took hers.

"My Joe," she said, "give your mama a kiss." He bent over her bed and wrapped his arms around her, mindful of the tubes she was attached to. He told himself he wouldn't let her see him cry but he couldn't help it. The tears were flowing unbidden. He felt a slight tap on his shoulder. It was the doctor telling him to let her rest. As he was about to turn away she reached up a touched his cheek and smiled. As he left the room to wait outside, Bethany showed up. She wrapped her arms around him.

"It's my mother," he said.

"I know, Joe," she said, "I'm very sorry. She is at peace. She knows it is time and she is ready."

"But the doctor said her heart is getting stronger."

"I know but it is not to be. I was sent to assist her on her journey across the great divide."

Just then the doctor appeared, "I'm really sorry, Joe," he said, "she's gone." Bethany disappeared to help his mom. And although he was struggling in a dark place he was glad she was not alone.

He did not see Bethany for two weeks. "I wanted to allow you time to grieve in solitude," she said.

"Thanks," he said. "I guess Mom is now truly with the angels. I failed her, you know."

"How so?"

"The only thing she wanted from me was for me to be married and give her grandchildren. I failed miserably."

"Maybe. But she knows it is because you never met the right woman."

"For me the right woman would have been like the one my dad married."

"Where did I hear that? Maybe you should look in the places your dad looked."

"Well, if you run into him, ask him where he looked and then tell me."

He was now totally alone. His father passed away five years prior, he was an only child and now his mom to whom he was devoted, was also gone. It took every bit of his strength to get back into writing. But, with help from Bethany, he was back in front of his computer and punching it. He was a third of the way through his book and he still had not settled on a way for his character to fall in love with an angel which was against the rules as Bethany pointed out.

One day Bethany told him they had reason to celebrate. She had served her time and was no longer on probation, which meant she could chose the human she wanted to be with for the rest of that human's life.

"Are you telling me I'm stuck with you for the rest of my life?" he said.

"Yeah, if you want me," she said.

"Do I have a say in this?" he asked.

"I don't know," she said. "Consider yourself lucky. Most humans don't even know who their angels are. They made an exception in your case. Don't ask me why because I don't know."

"You don't know a lot," he said.

"That's because I'm on the lowest rung of the ladder. Would you like me to be your forever angel?"

"Sure. You've saved me a couple times and you're easy on the eyes."

"Easy on the eyes?"

"Alright, you're a great looking woman. Plus, I'm used to you. What happens if I get a girlfriend?"

"Oh. I don't know how that will turn out. You think she might be jealous?"

"Or you," he said.

"No. I can't be jealous because we cannot have that kind of relationship. I'm here strictly to keep you out of trouble."

"Since we're on the subject," Joe said, "is there a male angel you might go for?"

"The only male angel I know is Mickey, and that could never happen. I really would like us to drop this discussion."

"Consider it dropped," he said. He could see she was becoming rattled.

Joseph had a meeting with his agent and when he returned home Bethany was sitting in his living room.

"I still can't get used to you coming and going whenever you please," he said.

"I have bad news," she said ignoring his comment.

"Are you in trouble again?" he asked but she said no. She was leaving him to do an errand of mercy. There was an old woman who was very sick but who refused to go. She just languished day after day unable to move or talk.

"I didn't think people had that choice," Joe said. He was thinking about his mother's sister, his aunt Dorothy who lingered for weeks before dying.

"It is not a conscious choice," Bethany said, "haven't you ever heard of people who linger on for a long time before accepting death?"

"So, they want you to push her over the edge?"

"Nothing like that. I am to bring peace to her and help her on her journey."

"Like you did with my mom." he said.

"Yes," was all she said and was gone. He wanted to ask her how long she would be away but he didn't get the chance. He wished she wouldn't be so abrupt.

CHAPTER SIX

Joseph's doorbell rang and it annoyed him because it caused the thought he was about to put into his computer, to slip from him. He was not expecting anyone but when he answered the door, he was looking at Bethany. He was very surprised. She had never rang his bell before and the thought that sprang to his mind was she had lost her powers. Was she being punished?

"Bethany," he said, "this is a surprise. Why did you ring the doorbell?"

"Aha. fooled you didn't I?" she said, "I just wanted to come in as a normal person."

"Bethany, ringing the doorbell does not make you a normal person," he said, "you can never be a normal person. You're an angel."

Lately, the vibes he was getting from her were, she wanted to be normal. He did not know if that were possible and he suspected she didn't know either.

She surprised him when she said, "I would like to meet your friend, Tony."

"Why?" he said. He was looking at her suspiciously.

"No reason. You talk to him a lot and spend time with him. I would like to know some of the people you know."

"Tony does not know you're an angel and I want to keep it that way."

"I'm okay with that. I just want to meet him. You can introduce me as someone you haven't seen in a long time. I promise I won't do anything to embarrass you."

He introduced her as a friend he knew in college and hadn't seen since then. He wanted to give her an occupation that she was knowledgeable about in case it came up in conversation. When Tony enquired about her last name Joe had to think fast but she beat him to it. "Templar," she said.

As a joke Tony said, "are you related to any of the Knights?" He was laughing when he said that but she was serious.

"I've been told that my family goes back to the Knights Templar." Joe was gazing at her. He didn't know she even knew about that organization.

"What do you do? Jobwise I mean," Tony said

"I'm a bereavement counsellor. I counsel people who have suffered a death in the family and are having a difficult time dealing with it. I was there for Joe when his mom passed."

Tony looked at his friend. "You never told me you were getting counselling," he said.

"I didn't want to spread it around," Joe said. Bethany sensed Joe was becoming tense so she engineered the conversation away from her by getting Tony to talk about his job as an author's agent. Eventually the men were discussing Joe's new book and some of the difficulties he was running up against. They were in a restaurant and when the server went over to get their drink orders Bethany said she was not much of a drinker so she ordered beer. Her eyes lit up in a smile when she looked at Joe who said he would like beer also. Tony agreed that beer all around would be fine. Between dinner and dessert Bethany excused herself to go to the ladies room and Tony took the opportunity to tell Joe, Bethany was hot. And he thought his buddy had hit the jackpot.

Later, Bethany said, "so Tony thinks I'm hot, huh."

"How do you know that? Were you standing there invisible?"

"No. I noticed how his eyes were roaming over me so I left to allow him to talk about me. Plus, the beer wanted to come out. I like him. How long have you known hm?'

"Since high school. We lost touch for a few years so, imagine my surprise when I saw his name in a writers manual as an agent. Would you like another beer?"

"No. I didn't like the beer. To me it was too bitter. I would like some champagne if you have it."

"I have champagne but I'm remembering your last experience with the bubbly."

"Don't worry I only want one glass. I will be okay with just one glass. Besides, I'm planning to stay over if you'll have me."

"You're welcome to stay. The nightgown is still in the closet."

Joseph finished his book and his publishers rushed it into print. They wanted to keep his name in the public's view. They called it striking while the iron is hot. But the book got Bethany into trouble. Mickey told her she should not have allowed Joe to have his character fall in love with an angel. She protested that she had no control over what Joe wrote but Mickey insisted part of her job was making sure he did not put out falsehoods about relationships between angels and humans. What he wrote could never happen even in fiction.

"So, you're back on probation?" Joe asked.

"No. He just yelled at me. I'm okay. But he's correct. I should have stopped you."

"You couldn't," Joe said, "I have something called free will and even an angel can't take that from me."

Joe brought up a subject he'd been ruminating for some time. "I want to take you shopping," he said, "so you'd have your own clothes and wouldn't need to keep borrowing from stores."

"Shopping?" she said, "that's very generous. I don't want you to spend a lot of money."

"Don't worry about the money," he said, "do you want to go shopping?"

"Yes. Thank you."

The shopping expedition occurred two days later. Their first stop was to a high end boutique where she bought two gowns that could be worn for special occasions similar to the charity ball.

Next, they went to a mall where she purchased everyday clothes including nightwear, underwear and shoes. They were passing a jewelry store and Joe spied a necklace in the window. He put his hand on her arm and pointed to the necklace.

"Oh, no," she said, "it's beautiful but I'm sure it is very expensive."

"Come on," he said, "let's check." Fifteen minutes later they left the store with the necklace.

As she was unpacking her purchases she said, "Joe, I feel like a kept woman."

"No need to feel that way," he said, "this is in return for your services. You kept me from making mistakes twice and you've helped me elevate my writing. My books are selling because of your intervention. You even helped with the last one that you got into trouble over, by not stopping me and look how it's selling. The reports claim having my character fall in love with an angel adds spice."

"Since you put it like that, I accept." She left after that and he went into the guest room to find she had hung up her clothes in the closet. He also noticed the nightgown from his earlier girlfriend was missing. She had folded it and put it into a drawer of the dresser.

Tony called Joe to tell him his publishers were hoping he had already started on a new book. They had this strike while the iron is hot mentality and were curious. Joe confessed he had not thought about another book yet and Tony's answer was his usual, Joe needed to get his butt in gear. Tony asked about Bethany. He wanted to know where she lived.

"Among the stars," Joe answered.

"Alright, alright," Tony said, "you don't have to tell me. Just don't let her distract you."

Joe was not sure what happened to Bethany when she disappeared. He assumed she simply spread herself on the wind like the ancient Greek gods. But he noticed she spent more time as a visible being. In that case she needed a place. He gently mentioned she could move in with him and got a resounding, "no. That is impossible."

"Well then," he said, "you could get an apartment, a small one and I would cover your expenses."

"You're pushing me toward being a kept woman," she said. "if I'm going to get an apartment, I should get a job."

"That would mean you have less time for me," Joe said, "isn't that why you came into my life in the first place?"

"Maybe but living with you is not the answer," she said.

Another idea slapped him in the face. He could pay her so she could have the means to maintain an apartment. He mentioned it and got silence from her. He thought, for a moment, she was going to disappear but she didn't.

"That could work," she said, "if I agree can we work out the details later? I'll have to convince Mickey it is for your benefit. Angels always have to consider their wards first."

"When will you discuss this with Mickey?" Joe asked.

"Now," she said and was gone. He once again made a mental note to talk to her about her abrupt disappearances. Many times, it happened while he was thinking of something else he wanted to say. She showed up that same evening and as soon as he saw her face he knew the news was not good. She did not bother using the door. She just materialized in his living room.

CHAPTER SEVEN

Her boss had said no to the arrangement. To him it appeared she and her human were getting too close, almost like in his book and he could not sanction it.

"Then, resign," Joe said.

"Resign? Angels cannot resign when you're an angel it is for all eternity," she said.

"Mickey is acting like a tyrant," Joe said.

Bethany rushed to his defense. "No," she said, "he is not a tyrant. He has to follow rules."

"I said he was acting like a tyrant," Joe replied, "rules can be broken or at least bent a little. I would like to talk to him. Is that possible?"

"I don't know," she said, "I can ask him"

"Isn't there a rule he has to comply with a human's request for an audience?"

"Okay," she said and disappeared. She didn't return.

Joe was going over some notes in his office when his doorbell chimed. He opened the door and it was Mickey standing on his mat.

"Why did you bother to ring?" Joe said.

"I wanted to get a human perspective," Mickey said, "I even took a taxi here."

"Come in," Joe said. He didn't expect such a quick response from Mickey so he had not prepared what he wanted to say. He decided he would have to wing it. Mickey opened the conversation.

"I'm told you think I'm a tyrant," he said.

"She told you that, eh. Well, I said you were acting like one. I should know, I write about tyrants all the time."

"I'm not your adversary, Joseph," Mickey said, "may I call you Joseph?" Joe waved his hand in agreement. "but we do have rules that must be followed."

"Fair enough," Joe said, "have you heard of free will?" That stopped Mickey momentarily. "Doesn't it apply to angels also?"

"Are you saying it is what she wants?"

"Yes, and you can be assured we are not breaking the no angel and human relationship rule. I have come to depend on her and I consider her a friend. Isn't that what you intended when you sent her here? How can she possibly help me if we are not friends?"

Mickey got up to leave. "I'm always amazed how astute some humans can be. I'll see myself out."

"Where is she?"

"I have no idea. Probably right here, listening." This time he walked through the door. So much for the human perspective. Joe expected Bethany to materialize as soon as Mickey was gone but he was disappointed. She waited until that evening to make her appearance.

"I heard everything," she said, "Mickey is right on. You are very astute and very convincing."

His next job was to find her an apartment. But before he could start looking they needed to fill out an application. And the application had to show a steady income at a good company. Putting 'angel' in the space reserved for employment was not going to cut it, even if she did put in three hundred years, in the space reserved for length of employment.

They worked at it most of the night stopping only for a quick dinner. Bethany was a secretary, had worked for A. Ward Inc. for five years and had steady employment. She was earning enough to be able to pay her rent on time and had the move-in money in her bank. She also had some investments in another account. Her reference would be Joseph Sommers the well-known author. Joe called Tony the next day and told him that Bethany was employed by A. Ward Inc. which was Anthony himself. If he received a call to verify her employment he should reply in the affirmative.

Tony wondered what happened to her job as a grief counsellor. Joe had forgotten about this earlier ruse so he had to think fast and told Tony she had quit that job because it paid very little. She was now working for him but to get an apartment in a nice neighborhood she needed to show steady employment for a few years. Tony gave him another idea.

"Why go through all that mess," Tony said, "why not buy a condo and lease it to her. You can afford it."

"I may end up doing just that," Joe said, "thanks for the idea. I should have thought of that."

"Your job is to write," Tony said, "and you do that very well."

When Bethany came to Joe's apartment, he told her his new idea, which Tony had given to him. She asked if that would suit them better.

"It would," Joe said, "no need for an application,"

"So, I would be working for you and renting an apartment from you," she said.

"Yes," he said, "does that bother you?"

"No," she said, "it sounds good to me. When do I start?"

"As soon as I buy an apartment," he answered. "And I'll choose one that's already furnished."

Joe took Bethany to look at apartments with him and it was love at first sight with the first apartment she saw. Joe wanted to look at others but she was adamant the first one she saw was what she liked. If he valued her opinion then that was the apartment she wanted. The agent told Joe it was the easiest sale she ever made and Joe admitted he, too, liked the apartment. The furnishings were top of the line and all the appliances looked new. They settled on a price and two days later Joe helped Bethany move her clothes into the apartment.

"I would like you to take me shopping one more time," Bethany told Joe.

"You need more clothes?"

"No," she said, "I would like a book to learn how to cook modern dishes."

"You really are planning to adapt to a human lifestyle." Joe said.

"As much as I can," she replied.

Her adaptation was going well until she was called away. She showed up at Joe's apartment with a sad expression to tell him she was going away for what might turn into a few weeks.

"I don't understand," Joe said, "I thought you were my forever angel."

"I am," she replied, "that means no other angel will be assigned to you, but I have other responsibilities. There is an unborn child who is severely ill and the parents are conflicted as to whether or not they should terminate the pregnancy."

"What can you do?"

"I don't know yet. My mission is not clear to me yet. I do know I will be assuming human form and be a counsellor"

"Can you make the child whole?"

"That is not in my power. The doctors think there may be a way to change the outcome, but it will take a miracle. That's where I would come in. My job will be to guide them without them having knowledge of it/"

"Why you? You told me there are as many angels as the number of people who have walked the earth."

"This is true but I possess the unique ability to bring calm into a situation. The parents are in great distress. My job is twofold. I have to let the parents see that the outcome outweigh the risks. The doctors may be able to save the child but if the parents refuse the operation, the child will almost certainly be stillborn. And I have to bring calm to the doctors so they can do their job with steady hands"

"When are you leav...?" Joe was asking when she intended to leave but she was already gone. In midsentence. Given her reason for leaving he felt guilty for wanting her to stay with him when he really did not need her. He wanted to apologize for his selfishness but she was gone, maybe for weeks. He turned his attention back to his book. In the beginning there was no deadline, now one was looming in front of his eyes. And that was because Tony had opened his big mouth and told the publishers what he was working on. And he didn't have Bethany at his elbow pushing. He was napping on his sofa when he felt a presence. It was Bethany. She looked at him with pity in her eyes.

"Sleeping on the job," she said, "I can't believe it. I leave on an errand of mercy and come back to find you sleeping on the job. I can wager all the tea in China you are behind on your deadline."

"Why, Bethany," he said, "welcome back. Good to see you too."

"Your sarcasm just rolls off my back. And since you asked, everything is well. The operation was a success and the parents now have a baby boy. He is a little frail but he will recover."

"That is good news," Joe said, "and now you're back to crack the whip, I'm sure I will make deadline. I'm going to be bold and give you credit. Do you think I would lose readership if I said I was helped by an angel?"

"I don't see how," Bethany said, "they liked it when you had your character fall in love with an angel. If you declare you have your own personal angel they just might be flocking to buy your book."

"Or they just might be sending in the guys with straitjackets."

CHAPTER EIGHT

Joe bought her a cookbook with dishes from all over the world, as a gift. When he presented to her, her eyes grew wide and a bright smile spread across her face. She opened her arms at the same time as he did and they enveloped each other with a tight embrace. They both stepped back at the same time.

"Sorry," Joe said, "I um..."

"It was as much my fault," Bethany said.

"Are you going to be in trouble?" Joe asked.

"I don't know. We weren't supposed to do that," she said.

"Mickey probably didn't notice," he said.

"Oh, he noticed," she said, "he has millions of eyes and ears all over."

"Well, blame it on me. Say I'm the one who grabbed you and you had nothing to do with it."

"I can't," she said, "that would be a lie."

Bethany's boss turned a blind eye to what occurred between her and the writer but he determined to keep a close watch on them. He would not intervene until he saw signs of them taking their relationship deeper. She invited Joe to dinner at her place. She went through her new cookbook and chose the simplest recipe which was roasted chicken which she served with corm and mashed potatoes. Joe told her he would bring the wine so she need not try to find a good one. But instead of wine he brought champagne because he knew she liked it. Also, it didn't matter if she drank a little too much since she was at her own home.

She was a little nervous about getting everything just right but she needed not worry because Joe enjoyed whatever she put in front of him and said so. He must be easy to please, she thought, and for the first time wondered why he had not been snapped up by some female. She also realized those were not the thoughts an angel should be having.

Bethany wanted Joe to give her more work. She was of the opinion she was not working enough to deserve her income. She proposed to him she should go out into the world and get a job but he was not comfortable with such a proposal. The idea struck him he could try her at proofreading his work. He currently used a proofreader and if Bethany could do it why not use her instead. He had planned to get a new computer with all the latest bells and whistles. He did that and gave his old, but serviceable, one to Bethany. He taught her how to use it and told her he was planning to have her proofread his work. She was excited about getting into something new.

Bethany surprised him by becoming adept at using the computer in an afternoon. But he wanted to know if she could adequately proofread his work. He devised a plan to test her, with her agreeing to it. He pulled out the files of an earlier book that had already been published and deliberately misspelled words, dropped punctuations and letters and made a mess of a chapter of the manuscript. He sent the file to her and told her to take her time proofreading it. He sent her the file that evening and to his surprise she sent it back the next morning with all the corrections. Not only that, she found two typos that had slipped through everybody including the publishers' people. The book was out there with the typos, and this he knew happened more often than authors liked to admit. Bethany had presented a manuscript that was totally perfect. Joe had found the ideal proofreader.

As he turned out chapters he sent them to her to be proofed and they came back to him in record time devoid of mistakes. Bethany was a gold mine. He floated the idea she could expand into proofing other writers' work since he was not able to keep her busy. She liked the idea as long as it was not necessary to meet with these people. Joe assured her that all negotiations could be done at arm's length by computer or telephone. So, just like that, Guaranteed Proofreading was born. She offered an ironclad guarantee that if there was just single mistake then the work was free. Those pesky typos which were a bane to writers could never slip past her.

Joe helped by referring other authors to her and soon Guaranteed Proofreading was a moneymaking business. The first thing Bethany did when she accumulated enough money was expand her wardrobe. She soon acquired a keen eye for the latest fashions and made Joe proud when they went out together. The lines were beginning to blur for Joe. He found himself not knowing who was the lady with him. Was she still the angel who was sent to help him or the fashion model she was fast becoming. He had to call her on it but was not sure how she would take it.

"Bethany," he said, "we need to talk."

"Yes," she said, "I know."

"You know?" he said.

"Yes. I can see it in your face. I have allowed the human aspect of me to become dominant. And that should not be. I am still your angel but lately I have been acting less so."

"I share a little of the blame," he said, "I've taken you places to show you off. And that is using you. I'm sorry. That is not why you were assigned to me."

"Shall I return the clothes I've bought?"

"No, no. Keep them. There will be times when you will wear them but maybe not so often."

"What should I do with the money from my business. It is in the account you started for me. I don't need all that money."

"I have an idea," Joe said, "we can start a charity and you can donate money on a regular basis."

"I like that," she said, "what charity?"

"We'll form one," he said," how about the Society of Angels? It will use the money to fund organizations who work among the poor of the world."

"Yes. That's where angels do their best work."

Bethany's proofreading business was a success. Guaranteed Proofreading had spread like wildfire across the publishing world so much so, she had to turn away business or she would have no time for Joe who was her reason for being there. Mickey summoned her for a meeting. He wanted to know why she had started a business since angels were not known to be business people. But he was mollified when she pointed out the money was going toward helping the poor people of the world. Mickey questioning her reminded her she had not received anything from Joe in about a month. He should have sent in at least one chapter but there was nothing from him. She braced him in his office.

"Don't tell me you have writer's block again," she accused him..

"Maybe I have," he said, "why do you ask?"

"I have not seen anything from you," she said.

"Oh, that," he answered, "I'm working on something. You'll get it soon."

Upon hearing this, she told him it was obvious she was negligent in her first job which was to push him. So, she intended to spend more time with him. This was not what he wanted because he was becoming attracted to her and the more time she spent with him the more difficult it became for him to think of her as his angel.

Joe was in his study when a man appeared at his elbow. It startled him since he didn't hear the man enter.

"Who are you?" Joe asked, "how did you get in here? I'm sure I locked that door."

"My name is Daniel and I came through the door. I'm Bethany's replacement."

"What? Replacement? I didn't ask for a replacement."

He was given a replacement for Bethany because their relationship was growing beyond the bounds of that of an angel and a human.

"No, you didn't but it was thought to be best," Daniel said.

"Well, no disrespect to you Daniel, but I don't want a replacement for Bethany."

"You don't have a choice in who is your angel. You could, of course, refuse an angel completely."

"Then, that's my choice," Joe said, "I am refusing an angel." As soon as he said that Daniel disappeared. He thought this was Mickey's doing. He knew that man was trouble the moment he laid eyes on him. He corrected himself. That angel was trouble. The problem he now faced was how to get Bethany back. He had told Daniel he did not need an angel but what he meant was he did not need an angel unless that angel was Bethany. But she was gone and once again he was alone.

CHAPTER NINE

Joseph Sommers, well-known author, was having difficulty concentrating on his art and it was suffering. His friend and agent, Anthony, talked to him about it, telling him his publishers were very dissatisfied and were making noises about dropping him.

"You need to get your butt in gear, my friend," Tony said, "if you don't meet the new deadline, I'm afraid there will be nothing I can do to prevent them from dropping you." Tony did not mince words so Joe knew he had to buckle down and finish the novel and stop feeling sorry for himself. He had no desire to start the process of finding a new publisher.

Late one night as he was preparing for bed his doorbell rang. He had no idea who could be calling so late so, surprise bloomed on his face when he opened the door to Bethany. He forgot the rules and threw his arms around her and she returned a tight hug.

"I know that's not allowed, but I couldn't help myself," he said. "I thought you were gone forever."

"I was," she said, "but you turned down another angel and you need help, so here I am. And I've brought my whip."

"You won't need it," he said, "I don't know how I did it but I finished the book."

"Have you sold my apartment?" she asked.

"No. It's still there. I was hoping you would return."

Joe and Bethany talked late into the night and he invited her to use the guest room and the nightgown she had put away. He encouraged her to resurrect her proofreading business and her first client was Joe.

His new book needed her proofing skills so he uploaded it onto her computer. The next day she returned to her apartment and started work on his book. Tony was pleased his favorite author was back in business and seemed to have his old inspiration on full throttle. He knew nothing about Joe's relationship with Bethany because his friend was always reluctant to talk about her and Tony never pressed him. But Tony realized Joe was at his best when she was around. He wondered why Joe didn't marry her and make the relationship permanent. She was beautiful and she was smart, what more could he want?

Bethany told Joe she had been studying a recipe and she would like to have him for dinner. She also extended an invitation to Tony and his lady friend, if he had one.

"He is seeing someone," Joe said. "Her name is Laura Bentley. She is an attorney. I will let him know. What are you planning to serve."

"A pot roast," she answered, "with those little potatoes."

He told her he would bring the wine. Although her preferred beverage was champagne, wine was more acceptable for dinners. Joe offered his help and she told him she would like him there while she was preparing the meal, just to make sure she didn't make any mistakes.

Tony and Laura arrived right at appointed hour and after introductions Laura complimented Bethany on her apartment.

"I love the furnishings," Laura said, "they're exquisite."

Bethany caught the slight shake of Joe's head before she answered, "I can't take credit for the furnishings," she said, "they came with the apartment."

"I'm an attorney," Laura said, "what is your business, Bethany? By the way your name is both unusual and beautiful. It sounds almost poetic."

"Thank you for the compliment. I have a small business called Guaranteed Proofreading. I proofread manuscripts before they go to publishers."

"And she is the best," Tony spoke up, "she even guarantees her work is error free or it is free to the author."

"Really. You're that sure of your skills," Laura said, "you must have an angel looking over your shoulder."

Bethany's head snapped up. "What did you say?"

"It's just an expression," Joe cut in.

"Of course," Bethany said and added, "I probably do."

The dinner was superb and the conversation went back and forth with the two couples enjoying each other's company. Joe knew Bethany had little experience with wine and noted how much she was taking in. She knew this and smiled at him to say 'don't worry. I'm taking it easy.' Laura brought up Bethany's last name much to Joe's dismay, because she really didn't have one but she remembered the one she had made up for Joe a long time ago.

"If you think her first name is unusual," Tony said, "wait until you hear her last."

"Templar," Bethany said and nothing else. But Tony did not let it drop.

"It's an ancient name," he said, " and it may go as far back as the Knights Templar."

"That's quite a pedigree," Laura said.

"Maybe," Bethany said, "I use only Bethany."

Soon Tony and Laura were saying goodnight and thanking Bethany for her hospitality. After they left Joe helped her in the kitchen with cleanup duties. Then they sat on the sofa with a glass of sherry to wrap the evening.

"If I had a guest room I would offer it to you," she said.

"No. no," he said, "I'll grab a cab and be home in no time."

"Of course," she said, "I can take the sofa and let you have the bed. The sofa is too short for you."

"A kind offer indeed," he said, "but I won't deprive you of your bed. I'm not sure I mentioned this but dinner was excellent and you did it all yourself."

"You being here gave me confidence," she said and added, "I don't think Laura is committed to Tony." He stopped midway between the kitchen and the living room when she said this and waited for more. He had long ago learned to take Bethany seriously when she spoke like that.

"What did you sense?" Joe asked.

"Her general demeanor when she spoke to him and the way she looked at him. I sensed he has a rival."

She had just dumped a problem squarely in his lap. He knew Tony loved Laura and even confided in him he was contemplating asking her to marry him. His angel had just put him on the horns of a dilemma. Tony was his best friend and he could not stand by and watch him walk into a heartbreaking situation. Bethany had to give him more but it was best if they left it for the next day.

He spent a sleepless night and called Bethany when he was sure she was up. He invited her for breakfast at his place.

"How fast you need me? she asked, "taxi or immediate."

"Immediate," he replied and before the word had left his mouth she was standing in front of him. He fixed a full breakfast with everything he had and when he laid it in front of her she said something that took his breath away.

"You know you'd make some woman a good husband with this cooking."

"I noticed you didn't say angel," he said, "no, forget I said that. I want to talk about Tony and Laura." She pointed out that humans like the phrase 'a marriage made in Heaven.' This one wasn't.

"Why?"

"There is another man in the picture for whom she cares deeply, and Tony doesn't know."

"How do you..." he started to ask and stopped, "of course you know." He did not want to brace his friend and risk losing his friendship but he had to find a way to allow Tony to find out for himself. The answer came to him, if she would go along with it. He could use Bethany's ability to see things mere mortals could not. But he had to come up with a workable plan before he tried to get her involved.

"Yes, I will help," she said.

"How did you know what...?"

"Seriously, Joe?"

"Sorry. Foolish question," Joe said.

His idea, which he ran by her, was to get Laura to tell Tony about her involvement with another man. Bethany agreed it was a good idea but it would take a lot of cunning to pull it off.

"That's your department," Joe pointed out.

"Not really," she replied, "I cannot lie and I cannot trick people."

"Okay," Joe said, "I'll do the planning. I write this stuff for a living."

The plan was ingenious in its simplicity. Bethany would go to Laura's office, pretend she had an appointment in the area, and invite Laura to lunch. During lunch she would use her natural persuasive ability to get Laura to admit to Tony she was in love with another man. It involved a small lie but Bethany thought it was necessary to save Tony from making a dreadful mistake.

Laura was surprised to see Bethany but accepted the lunch invitation.

Bethany was in Joe's office going over some corrections to his manuscript when his phone rang. It was Tony. He covered the phone to whisper to Bethany.

"It's Tony. He sounds distraught." The conversation was short. Laura had admitted to Tony she was in love with another man and was breaking things off with Tony.

"Our plan worked," Joe said, "although Tony is going to need some help to get over her."

CHAPTER TEN

Joe's book was released and was not as well received as his previous one. One critic wrote it seemed the author's muse had departed. Joe admitted to Bethany it was not his best work. He thought of abandoning the project more than once but Tony's advice was to send it on to the publishers. Now, he regretted doing that. Bethany pointed out this meant he had to write another great book so his readers would not be left with disappointment. And, she also pointed out, the sooner the better.

It didn't take Tony long to find a replacement for Laura but he promised himself this time he would tread cautiously.

"Should I invite Tony and his lady over so I can check her out?" Bethany asked.

"No," Joe replied, "let them fend for themselves, for now. Maybe they might discover if they are not suited for each other on their own."

"What about you, Joe?" she asked.

"If you're asking what I think you're asking," Joe said, "the woman I want is not available to me."

"Yes," she said.

"Let me ask you the same question," Joe said, "do you feel the need..."

She held up her hand to stop him. "Normally, angels do not feel that need. But I've been living like a human for long enough for me to have human feelings even though they are forbidden."

They both decided to table that particular discussion for another time, but Joe was not sure when would be an appropriate time. Bethany was called away to spend time with the distraught parents of a child who was dying of cancer. The child had slipped into a coma which meant death was near but the parents, especially the father, were inconsolable. Bethany was needed to bring a small slice of comfort to the couple. She promised Joe she would be back as soon as she was no longer needed. Joe expected her to be gone a long time.

She returned a month later. She had helped the child on her journey and had stayed with the parents until she felt they were beginning to heal. Joe had started a new project and she was anxious to read what he had written.

"No angels this time?" she asked.

"Nope. This is pure crime. Good guys against bad guys."

Joe kept at it with fervor. He was turning out pages at a high rate, as if he were possessed with a need to reconcile with his readers. Tony read the manuscript and declared Joe had hit one out of the park .He had no doubt the publishers would be pleased and he thought there was a larger than usual advance coming to Joe. If the publishers did not agree he would shop the book around. But he didn't have to. The publishers recognized they had a blockbuster in the making and did not want to lose out. They gave Joe a substantial advance and scheduled the earliest publication date they could manage.

The book sold millions of copies and was translated into five languages. Then Tony called with the news any author longed to hear. He had received a call from a Hollywood producer who was interested in acquiring the rights to make a movie of the book so, Joe and Tony arranged to go to Hollywood to meet with the producer and his staff.

When Bethany heard about their plans she offered to go with them as Joe's secretary but he told her it would not be a good idea, since he did not need a secretary. He returned from his meeting with the producers, quite elated. They had negotiated a large fee for his book and he was a happy man. All that was required was his signature on the contract. Bethany asked to see the contract. This surprised Joe. "Why?" he said, "our attorney has already given us the green light. But you're welcome to look it over."

Bethany's face clouded over as she read the contract. "Does your attorney have any experience dealing with film people?" she asked.

"No. He's Tony's friend and a corporate attorney. But he's worked with contracts. A contract is a contract and he said this is a normal contract."

"Joe, can you wait a few days before signing?" Bethany said. "I have a feeling this is not in your best interest."

"Why wait, Bethany?" he said, "they want to move on this as soon as possible."

"I understand," she said, "please, Joe, just a few days. I have to leave for a few days. You can sign when I get back."

"Okay, I guess a few days won't hurt ."

Tony was not happy with the hold up but Joe was adamant he wanted a few days to think about what he was signing. When Bethany returned, she asked to see the contract again. She held it up in front of Joe.

"They're planning to cheat you," she said. "Your book is worth five times what they plan to give you."

"How? How do you know this?"

"I heard them talking. They think you and Tony and your lawyer are inexperienced in film contracts so they can get your book at one fifth its value."

"That's where you were?"

"Yes. Get a new attorney who knows the film business."

Tony was skeptical about Joe's request to hire a more experienced attorney.

"This is no reflection on your friend," Joe said, "but I have it on good authority we're being taken. I am not signing until an experienced attorney says it is okay."

Tony came back a few days later and sheepishly agreed the film company was trying to cheat them. "I ran the contract by a law firm with experience in the film industry and they said this production company is noted for buying content on the cheap. They make a lot of money on their films, partly because they take advantage of authors. If they want your book they have to pay a lot more. Time to renegotiate. Your hunch was right on."

"I owe you big time," Joe told Bethany. "I've signed a contract for five times what they originally offered.'

"Thank you," she said, "but I don't need money."

"Give it to your charity," Joe said.

Bethany was thrilled she was able to prevent Joe from making a big mistake. She'd never known a human who needed protection more than Joseph Sommers. The man was his own worst enemy although he would never admit it. He needed protection from himself and she was glad to provide it.

CHAPTER ELEVEN

Joe and Bethany were just finishing dinner, enjoying a glass of sherry when he got her attention. "Beth, do you know anything of your former life?"

"Oh no," she said, "I have no former life. I was always an angel."

"Do angels age?"

"No. A hundred years from now I will be just as you see me now. But you will be..." she hesitated.

"You can say it. I will be dead."

"Why are we discussing this, Joe?"

"In my new book there will be a character who is the reincarnation of an Indian princess."

"A princess from India?"

"No. An American Indian Princess of the Chippewa tribe, who lived in a village on the shores of Gitchee Gumee."

"Would you like me to do research on this princess? You know I can travel through time."

Bethany stood still in a stand of trees and watched as Princess Snowbird of the Chippewa and three other young girls bathed and frolicked in the big lake. They stopped and dressed quickly when they heard shouting coming from their village. Presently a band of Indians from another tribe surrounded the women and were intent of taking them captive. The women ran but arrows rained down on them, killing them instantly. Bethany's eyes clouded over when she saw this but there was nothing she could do. She was witnessing an event that had already taken place.

She reported to Joe how Snowbird had died and how helpless she felt.

"You could not interfere," Joe said, "or you would have changed history. But thank you for that information. Now, I know how I can use Princess Snowbird in my book. You know I like to include a bit of historical fact in my books even though I write fiction."

"What role does she have?" Bethany asked.

"She is reincarnated in one of my characters and wreaks havoc on a group of people, who are the descendants of that tribe that attacked her village and killed her. It's part fantasy, part science fiction, part mystery and all action."

Now that Joe knew how Snowbird died, he was able to move ahead with his story and Bethany loved the way pages were flying out of his computer and landing in hers for her to proofread. Joe turned on the television to get the news and the first pictures that came up were about a hostage situation that was in progress. A man robbed a bank and took a cashier, a young girl, hostage. He was demanding a private plane to take him to a country that did not have an extradition treaty with the US. Bethany stopped to watch with Joe. The man's face was plastered all over the screen.

"I can help," Bethany said.

"You? How?" Joe said, "they have a professional negotiator there and that guy is not budging."

"He is desperate and he is dangerous," Bethany said, staring at the face on the screen. "He won't back down. If they rush him, they will kill him but the girl will be dead."

"What can you do?" Joe said.

"I will jam his gun so it won't fire," she said and disappeared. He was glued to the television to see what she intended. He saw the negotiator put his phone to his ear. He could not hear what was being said but the man raised his hand to tell the police to stand down. "The police was just told to hold up," the announcer said. "A female voice, probably the hostage, said the man wanted to surrender."

As Joe watched, the door of the bank opened and a gun was thrown out, then the young woman ran out with tears streaming down her face. The police closed in on the door and took the man into custody as soon as he came out. Just then Bethany materialized in the apartment.

"Well done," Joe said, "Nobody got hurt and the bank still has all its money. Was the girl in danger?"

"The girl was in grave danger. When he thought the police was going to break in he pointed the gun at her and pulled the trigger. But the gun didn't fire because I had jammed it. He should be punished for attempted murder. You should find a way to let the police know he tried to kill her."

"Is it still jammed?"

"It is and will be, until somebody fixes it. You're the expert on crime. I know you will think of a way to alert the police."

Joe could not tell the police that the teller's life was saved because an angel jammed the man's gun. He had to find another way to let the authorities know they should add attempted murder to their list of charges. An idea came to him and he put it into play immediately without consulting Bethany.

The police received a call from a concerned citizen who was calling from a pay phone. He had it on good authority the teller was saved because the gun jammed. The man tried to shoot her so attempted murder should be added.

"Who is calling?" the cop asked, "and how do you know this?"

"A concerned citizen. Tell the authorities to check the gun." The concerned citizen hung up.

The police chief called a news conference to announce they were adding attempted murder to the charges of bank robbery and kidnapping. By a wonderful accident the gun jammed or the young lady would have been killed.

Joe's publishers decided to send him on a tour to whip up interest in his new book. And that brought up the problem of how to include Bethany. When he asked her if she wanted to go, she answered in the affirmative without even thinking about it. She could travel along cloaked in invisibility and appear only when they were alone but neither wanted this. He floated the idea to his publishers that she travel as his companion who was coming along for the adventure. They didn't mind but they were not okay about paying her way. They gave it their blessing when he told them she would fund her adventure herself. They did, however, ask if she were his love interest. His vague answer did not satisfy them but it told them it was none of their business and they should drop it. They did.

Since the tour was only to cities in the Northeast section of the country, Joe elected to drive rather than fly. To him it was less wear and tear on him than if he were constantly running to catch flights. And it was easier to tell himself he was traveling with a beautiful lady with the occasional stop to talk about his book. Bethany was brimming with excitement to be introduced to the world of publishing. She was astounded at how many people turned out to hear Joe and to get his autograph. Not for the first time she regretted being hampered by her life as an angel. This was a man she could dearly love, now that she had come to know that feeling.

Midway through the tour Joe sensed Bethany was having some problems with their arrangement. So, he asked her about it.

"I am not comfortable with you being the center of attention of all those attractive ladies," she said. "I think most of them are more interested in you than your book."

"Why, Beth," he said, "if I didn't know better I would say you're jealous."

"Don't be ridiculous," she said, "angels can't be jealous."

"That may be true," he said, "but I think you're getting to be more human than angel."

"This discussion is closed," she said and disappeared. Damn, he thought how could he have a worthwhile discussion with someone who keeps disappearing? But the genie was out of the bottle. She was jealous and he had no idea how to deal with it. But he admitted to himself she was having the same feelings he had been tamping down in himself. He fell in love with her a long time ago but kept it to himself. If she were having similar feelings, they were in for a troublesome future. No question about it, she would be taken away from him.

As they were walking back to their hotel the next evening, after dinner at a restaurant, Bethany broached the subject.

"You were right, Joe," she said, "I am jealous of those women and I don't know what to do about it. I've never encountered this before."

"You should know, Beth," he said, "those women's interest is not reciprocated. I see them only as fans."

"Perhaps I should leave the tour," she said, "then I wouldn't be faced with this on a daily basis.

"You could," he answered, "but we'll still have a problem to solve. Plus, I would miss you."

At the next stop, Bethany sat at the rear of the room and Joe could see her eyes roving over the crowd coming to light on every young attractive female. Was Bethany reading their minds? He wasn't sure she had that ability since it had never come up in conversation, but if she could it would be the source of her jealousy. He decided to test the bounds of their relationship. They were in the elevator alone going up to their rooms after dinner. "Why don't we share the same room for the rest of the tour?" he asked, "it seems pointless to have two rooms. We are friends after all."

She turned to look at him with surprise written all over her face. "The same room? And the same bed?"

"Well, most hotel rooms have two beds," Joe answered.

"You will be okay with that?" she said.

"Sure. If that is okay with you. Please don't disappear. You have a tendency to do that when a conversation becomes uncomfortable."

"I won't," she said, "can we talk more about this?

"Of course."

They talked a lot more about it with Bethany reminding him they were venturing into forbidden territory just talking about it. The big problem hanging over their heads like a sword was the rule that angels and humans could not have a relationship. They could not fall in love with each other. Joe wanted to know who made that rule and what would happen if it were broken.

"I don't know," she said, "to both questions."

"Who would know?" Joe said.

"Mickey, perhaps. But he has to follow rules too."

"Can you stop being an angel?" he asked, "can you live like a human, grow old and die? No more powers?"

"Now, you're entering a realm unknown to me. We need to talk to Mickey. He knows things other angels do not."

"Unfortunately, Mickey and I are not always on the same wavelength."

"Mickey admires you very much," Bethany said. "I promised not to disappear but I need to go to see him and ask him to come to you."

"Will you be here when I talk to him? I mean in human form?"

"Yes," she said, "I will be."

CHAPTER TWELVE

Bethany did not return that night. He went over to her room and knocked but received no answer. He was going over some notes for his session later that day when there was a knock at his door. He opened it to Bethany in the company of Mickey.

"Hello, Mickey," he said, reaching his hand for a shake, "welcome to both of you."

"Hello, Mr., er, Joseph," Mickey said.

"Come in, please," Joe said stepping aside. "Thank you for coming. I'm sure Bethany has already told you why I requested to see you."

"She has," Mickey responded, "and, if I may say so, it's a dilemma. I have never received such a request. This is all new ground for me too. If I understand her correctly, she wants to give up being an angel to become human, all because she has fallen victim to the human weakness of love."

"Hold on," Joe said, "we don't consider it a weakness." Joe felt compelled to defend his humanity. "We..."

Mickey held up his hand, 'No need to defend your humanness, Joe," he said, "forgive me. Wrong choice of words."

Joe waved his hands in a 'you're forgiven' gesture.

"I've always thought angels were immune to the feeling of romantic love," Mickey continued, "but Bethany has proved me wrong. Part of the blame lies with me for assigning a female angel to you."

"And I'm glad you did," Joe jumped in to let Mickey know where he stood. "Bethany has achieved goals with me where a male agent would have failed."

"Like falling in love with you."

"Yes. That too."

"And you with her," Mickey persisted.

"Also, true."

"The question now becomes, where do we go from here?" Mickey said. "Since this is all new to me, I am open to suggestions."

Up to that point Bethany had not said anything but her question caused Mickey to stop for a moment.

"Do you have the power to make me a complete human?" she asked.

Mickey turned his attention to her before answering, "I am not sure how much authority I have in this matter. I have never been tested before."

"Is there someone above you?" Joe wanted to know.

Mickey could not give a definitive answer to Joe's question. He launched into a somewhat convoluted discussion of the place angels held in the universe and their interaction with humanity since the beginning of time.

"I mean no disrespect, Mickey, when I say you have not answered my question."

"And I am not disrespecting you by being vague. The direct answer is, I don't know. I do have some authority so, maybe we should start there."

The basic question was, could Bethany cease to be an angel and become a human and after a long time they were not near an answer. So, Mickey proposed a compromise. He thought it was possible to find a middle ground. She would have to give up some power that meant nothing, like appearing and disappearing, or walking through walls. But since she had a business proofreading manuscripts she wanted to retain the ability to ferret out every mistake and typo. Mickey asked them a question that gave them pause.

"What happens if you discover you really aren't suited to each other. It happens, you know."

"Then we'll deal with it the way people have for thousands of years. What you probably don't know Mickey, is when there is love, there's always a way."

"Humans place great importance on growing old together," Mickey said, "would you like that?'

"Yes," Joe said. Mickey looked at Bethany and she nodded yes.

"Okay," Mickey said, "I can't be sure how successful I will be in granting your requests. You'll find out when Bethany tries to use an ability. For instance, the first time she tries to walk through a wall and her nose impacts with it."

"Will I see you again?" she asked him.

"No, Bethany, you won't have access to me. You and Joe will have to meet life as humans have done since they walked the earth."

Mickey was about to leave but Joe detained him. He wanted Bethany to be sure she wanted this.

"Beth, this is a lifechanging step for you. Are you sure you want this? You won't be able to see through my clothes."

Mickey held up his hand, "what's this about seeing through clothes?"

Joe related the time she saw through a man's female clothes and discovered she was a man. That saved Joe from a great deal of embarrassment.

"That's fine," she said, "I'll just have to wait until you take them off. I love you Joe, and I want to grow old with you."

Mickey walked to the door and waited for Joe to open it. "Probably might be the last act as a human," he said, stepped through the door and disappeared.

Bethany was standing in the middle of the room staring straight ahead. She looked at Joe and a smile covered her face. "There are many things you have to each me," she said.

"You'll find I am a very patient teacher," Joe said, "but I think you are a fast learner." He reached out to her and took her in his arms for the first time since they've known each other. She came to him willingly and turned her face to him. He placed his lips on hers and she opened hers to receive him. When they broke apart she was panting.

"You're a great teacher," she said.

"That's because I have a willing student," he said, "want to try that lesson again?"

"Yes, please," she said, "and I'm looking forward to other lessons you want to give." That night she informed the desk she was checking out of her room and moved in with Joe. His tour was a stunning success. When they returned home the first decision Joe had to make concerned the condo he had bought to house Bethany. She was moving into his apartment so he no longer needed it but he was not sure he wanted to sell so, he put it up for rent.

Bethany's proofreading business was flourishing since she had not lost the magic she had as an angel. One day, Joe told her to test her ability to walk through a wall but cautioned her to put her arms out just in case she no longer could. She did as he said and came up against an immovable wall. She had lost that ability.

"Can you see through my clothes?" he asked with a huge smile on his face. She looked him up and down before answering.

"Yes," she said, "I can see everything."

"Really? What color underwear do I have on?"

'You're not wearing underwear."

"You mean you can see my unmentionable?"

She threw her arms around his neck, "I'm teasing you," she said, "I cannot see through your clothes. That's gone too."

"Well, I am not sorry you lost that. Although it did give me some pleasant moments thinking my angel could see me naked."

Joe announced he was going to start something new after a short hiatus. "You can still crack the whip if I'm being lazy."

"I don't know if I could," she said, "now that I'm love with you."

Tony called to tell Joe he had met a new woman and she was a knockout. She was also a twin and he wanted Joe to meet the woman's sister. Joe took time to explain to his friend that meeting his girlfriend's sister was not an option since he was now committed to Bethany.

"When did this happen?" Tony asked.

"While we were on the tour," Joe answered, "but in truth I was falling for Beth for a long time. We decided, while we were on the tour, to admit our feelings for each other."

"That's great news, Joe," Tony said, "now I can stop worrying you're headed to a life of a lonely old man. You finally realized what an angel she is."

"I've known it for a while, Tony. It just took me a while to accept it."

CHAPTER THIRTEEN

The doorbell rang and Bethany went to open the door. Joe heard her say, "oh", and nothing more so, he went over to see what had made her become so tongue tied. Mickey was standing there.

"Hello, Mickey," he said, "this is a surprise. Come in. What brings you here?"

Mickey entered and immediately apologized for the interruption. "I know I said you won't hear from me again, but I am here on an errand of mercy."

There was a massive airplane crash when two planes collided killing everyone onboard except one little boy who was traveling alone to visit his grandparents That boy was now fighting for his life in a hospital. He was just hanging on by a thread refusing to accept death. His mother was in a panic and kept asking him not to leave them. Her will was so strong it kept the boy from crossing over but he was in increasingly terrible pain. Death would have been a release for him but she could not see it that way. Mickey wanted Bethany to go to her and bring her peace and understanding.

"But I'm not an angel anymore," she protested, "I no longer have that ability."

"I can give you back what you gave up, for this assignment," Mickey said.

"Like a part-time angel," Joe said.

"I prefer to look at it as an angel on call," Bethany said.

"Bethany, I'm here because you have demonstrated, over and over, the ability to bring healing to people who are hurting and both mother and son are hurting, The son physically and the mother emotionally. I want you to show the mother that she is preventing her son from leaving his pain behind. The doctors have told her he is now beyond their meager capabilities. Only death will bring him release. She refuses to accept it."

"I will go, Mickey," Bethany said, "Joe?"

"Of course," Joe said, "this is what made you an angel in the first place. I will never stand in your way of bringing healing to someone."

Bethany and Mickey walked over to the door and walked right through it. His angel was an angel again. Joe was searching the news programs to find anything he could about the plane accident and one headline screamed, LITTLE BOY WHO SURVIVED PLANE CRASH DIES. Bethany had done her job. She had convinced the boy's mother to let him go so she could find peace and the boy's pain would stop. Bethany helped the boy across the divide and then returned home.

Joe answered the door to find Bethany and Mickey there. "I've brought Bethany back," Mickey said, "take good care of her so, I could call her up again if the need arises."

"You've got it, Mickey," Joe said, "this lady is in good hands." He turned to Bethany after Mickey left.

"Are you an angel again?"

"Not fully," she replied, "an angel on call."

"That sounds like a good title for a book.," he said, sounding it out, " *An Angel On Call*, "

She told him she had a question for him. When he told her to go ahead, she asked him why he had never made a pass at her. Joe put aside the book he was reading and stared at her.

"Where did you get the idea of passes?" he asked her.

"From you," she answered. "In your last book a male character made a pass at a female character and eventually they ended up in bed."

"The only answer I have is, I was allowing you to absorb being human before moving on to other things."

"Well, I thoroughly enjoy kissing you and having you caress me so, I think I'm ready for other things."

"Okay, but they have to come up naturally. You cannot force them."

"Right," she said, "in one of your books you said something about the mood being right. Now, I understand what you meant. Being human is not as easy as I thought."

Bethany told Joe she wanted to go shopping by herself. She just wanted him to drop her off at the mall and come back for her later. He had no problem with this but he thought she should learn to drive a car. When she asked him to teach her he recommended she take lessons from a professional. She asked him why he couldn't do the job and it took him a long time to explain humans get into trouble when family members or friends try to teach each other to drive. He wasn't sure she completely understood his convoluted explanation but she accepted it and the subject was dropped.

"I would like to show you what I bought," she said, and went into the bedroom to change clothes before he answered. When she came out she was wearing a pink negligee with pink underwear which showed through the sheer fabric of the negligee. His pulse began to race and he immediately felt the pull to pick her up and take her to bed. Instead, he stared at her and one word left his lips, "wow".

She modeled other purchases but the negligee stayed with him. He didn't know how many years she existed as an angel but as a first time human, she possessed the ability to send a man's blood pressure soaring. Bethany the angel had disappeared and Bethany the deliciously appealing woman had taken her place. Her first outing as a shopper was a resounding success. She quickly learned to navigate the mall and to browse through stores until she found exactly what she wanted. When she saw the negligee on the mannequin she knew it would be wonderful eye candy for Joe and she nailed it. When she took it off she saw a little disappointment cross his face but he quickly recovered and showed interest in her other purchases.

Two nights later after they had enjoyed a meal she fixed using a cookbook and a little help from Joe. They were relaxing with a glass of champagne when Joe put his glass on the coffee table and took hers from her. He stared into her eyes and noticed for the first time they changed color as she moved her head. She was looking at him with anticipation written all over her face and they were bright blue. He reached for her and she came to him willingly and when he bent to her lips she parted hers to accept his tongue. The kiss lasted for an eternity as they melded into each other. Joe stood and without a word picked her up and carried her into the bedroom.

He put her on the bed and leaned over her to whisper, "I love you." Her eyes opened wide when she heard this and they turned into a light gray because they were being clouded with tears.

"Tears?"

"Happy ones. I've waited so long to hear you say that. I love you too. Angels miss so much."

That was the end of the conversation because Bethany could only groan when his hand roamed over body and landed on a breast. He opened her blouse and took it out and his mouth found it and she squealed in delight. This was her first time so he told himself he would take it slow with her but he could not help himself and very soon he had stripped her clothing away. When he turned to take his clothes off she gently moved his hands and did the job herself. The two naked bodies were entwined but not for long. Very soon he gave in to his desires and entered her.

Afterwards, spent but contented they fell asleep in each other's arms. Bethany giggled before she dozed off and Joe heard, "angels miss so much."

They both slept late and Joe was surprised to find they were still wrapped around each other, naked. Presently she awoke and looked at him and then at herself.

"Did we sleep naked?" she said.

"As a newborn," he answered.

"We don't have to get up, do we?"

"Not if we don't want to," he said.

"But I'm hungry," she said.

"Then we have to get up. Get dressed, I'm taking you out to breakfast."

He saw her put her hand out and walk to ward a wall only to have her fingers impact the hard surface.

"Still gone," she said.

"Until Mickey comes back to ask your help in another emergency."

"Does that bother you?"

"Of course not. I'm proud that I'm in love with a woman who can become an angel and comfort people in distress."

"Right now, this would-be angel is hungry," she said.

"And it is my assignment to feed her," Joe said.

There was a good breakfast place two blocks away so they elected to walk. It was a bright sunny morning in New York. The trees were all bright green and birds played among them. An elderly lady had her dog on a leash but the dog was straining at it to get close to Bethany and it finally broke free. The dog disregarded the woman's shouts and approached Bethany who stooped to rub its head. Contentment poured from the animal.

"He is never so sweet with strangers," the woman said, "I'm sorry he broke away."

"Don't be," Bethany said, "he looks very well-mannered."

"That's the first time he's ever done that," the woman said, "you must be some kind of angel."

Under his breath Joe murmured, "you don't know half of it."

As they were entering the apartment after breakfast Bethany told Joe she was expecting a novel for proofreading. She wondered if it had arrived while they were away. She fired up her computer and yelled out to Joe, "it's here. A long one too. I have to get to work."

Joe too, had to get to work to finish his novel so Bethany can get to it. That was one of the advantages of living with his proofreader.

CHAPTER FOURTEEN

Tony was still dating the woman he met recently, although he confided he sometimes felt they were pranking him. They looked so much alike that he was not always sure he was with the one he should be with. Joe advised him to find something only the one he wanted would have. Maybe something in her personality that was special to her. But a personality trait would be obvious only after they had sat down in a restaurant and begun a conversation. So, it was fairly easy to prank him. Another one of his authors asked him to recommend a good proofreader because the one he had was allowing too many errors to slip through. He knew Bethany was the best in the business but before he recommended her he wanted to know if she would be interested in more business. Joe told him the only way he could know that was to call her.

"Tony called today," Bethany said later, "he wanted to recommend me to another author. But I asked him not to because I have all the work I can handle. I don't ever want to get so busy I don't have time for you."

Mickey materialized in their living room. "Have you heard of knocking?" Joe asked, "if you keep showing up here, you may as well move in."

"Sorry, I can't fully appreciate your levity. I'm here to warn you."

"Warn me?" Joe said.

"Yes. There will be an intrusion to your home. I can't say more. I have already stepped over multitudes of bounds just to tell you that. Bethany, I'm giving you back your powers temporarily so you can help Joe." With that he disappeared.

"I appreciate the warning but he could have given us a time frame."

"He overstepped his authority just warning you." Bethany said.

They stayed up worrying when the intruders would arrive. Joe made sure the door was locked but the lower panel of the door was glass and it would be child's play for someone to break it and reach in to open the door. He had long since determined to get a more substantial door but never got around to it. Sleep finally forced them into bed and he was just dozing off when he heard glass shatter. He touched Bethany's shoulder and she came awake immediately.

"They're here," Joe said, "I don't have anything I could use as a weapon." Bethany disappeared and when his eyes roved around the room searching for a weapon, he saw a baseball bat leaning against the wall. He smiled because he knew he didn't own a baseball bat. He walked out of the bedroom just as two men were heading into his study.

"Hold it there," he shouted and the men stopped and turned in his direction. They had guns which they pointed at him.

"You got a bat and we got guns," one of them said, "who do you think is gonna win this matchup?"

Joe edged closer to them knowing Bethany would interfere. Both men raised their guns. "Stop right there, buddy," one said, "you'll be dead before you can raise that bat." A voice inside his head said, "keep going."

Both men fired but both guns jammed. As they were pulling the triggers Joe brought the bat down on one arm and then the other. The intruders screamed and went down holding their arms. Bethany came out of the bedroom rubbing her eyes, "what's going on?" she said.

"Call the police," Joe said, "these men tried to rob us."

"They're on the way," she said.

One of the robbers tried to get up but Joe put the bat to his head. "Don't move or I'll crack your skull."

"I'll be back," Bethany said and left the room, coming back with a bat which she put to the other man's head.

"You heard what he said," she told him, "and I'm stronger than he is so, your skull will shatter." Joe looked at her. Stronger? As angel Bethany she probably could muster enough strength to lift the world but as human Bethany, he didn't think so. But this was neither the time nor place to argue the point. And apparently the intruder didn't think so either. He just lay on the floor moaning and nursing his arm.

The police walked in through the open door. They hauled both men erect before calling ambulances.

"You two people are superman or something?" a uniform asked, "these guys had guns. All you had were bats but you wasted them."

"I think our guardian angel was watching over us tonight," Joe said.

"You can say that again," the cop said, "you need a stronger door."

The cops left at the same time as the ambulances.

"Pack an overnight bag," Joe said, "we're not staying here with a broken door. We'll spend the night in a hotel and first thing tomorrow I'm getting a new door."

They ended up staying two nights because it took two days to get the door fixed. They treated it as a mini vacation. They did not take their computers with them because they did not intend to do any work. It was two days of love making, dining out and sleeping late. Joe had broken the arms of both men so, not only were they facing breaking and entering, attempted robbery and attempted murder charges, they were dealing with the pain and suffering that come with broken limbs.

The police still could not understand how two people could face down criminals with guns. They examined the guns and found them to be in good working order. The men said their guns jammed. But the police did not believe them. The odds of both guns jamming were too long to give any credence to their story. At any rate, the criminals, should be thankful they were not facing murder charges.

"I wish we could find some way to thank Mickey for giving us a heads-up," Joe said.

"No need," Bethany replied, "he already knows we are thankful. I like our new door. Not only is it strong it is very stylish."

"Speaking of stylish," Joe said, "I would like to see you in your negligee. You know the one I'm talking about. You haven't worn it in a while."

"Oh, I can do that," she said, "while I'm putting it on, you get us some champagne. And then we'll just see what happens."

Life continued normally for Joe and Bethany until the day there was a knock on the door and when Bethany opened it Mickey entered.

"Oh, the head dude," Joe said, "welcome. What brings you to our door?"

"A matter of grave importance," Mickey said, "I need to borrow Bethany."

Joe was about to make a snide remark but Bethany held up her hand to stop him. Mickey continued to tell them why he was there. A man, Jason Samuels, was convicted of murder based on the testimony of Jean French who was paid a large sum of money to lie. Sentencing was set for the following month and it could be death or life in prison. Mickey wanted to insert Bethany into the situation to help Samuels. Her job was to get Jean French to retract her testimony, probably opening herself to perjury.

Jean French, a nondescript woman of fifty, was standing in line to pay for an expensive scarf at a high end boutique, when another woman approached her.

"A beautiful scarf," the stranger said, "I'm sure it is very expensive. You shouldn't spend all the money in one place."

"Excuse me?" Jean said and turned to look at the other woman who was not there. When she got to the cashier she placed the scarf on the counter and hurried away without saying a word. The cashier called out to her but she didn't turn around. Jean was shaking when she left the store. She had other errands to do but went straight home. She convinced herself her eyes were playing tricks on her and determined to forget about what happened in the store. But it was not easily done.

She had just turned on the television to watch a movie when she felt a presence and the woman from the store was sitting next to her.

"How did you get in here?" Jean asked. "Who are you?"

"That really does not matter," the stranger said, "but if you want a name, call me Conscience. That's my name."

"What do you want with me?"

"You and I are bound together and every time you try to spend the money you received for telling a lie in court, I will be with you." Then the stranger was gone. Jean decided to get the goods she wanted by another means. She ordered them to be delivered, But every time she dialed in an order Conscience was standing in front of her. Jean began to think she was losing her mind since she could not get rid of the stranger who seemed to materialize out of nowhere.

"Why are you haunting me?" she asked, "I haven't done anything to you."

"No, not to me, but to the man in prison. Your lies have put him there and he may be executed. I know exactly how much you were paid to lie. You cannot get rid of me. I will be with you as long as you live." Jean put her head in her hand as tears rained down her face.

"Please," she said, "I needed the money. I needed money."

"No one needs money enough to ruin another person's life. That is what you did. I will remind you of that every day."

"What can I do to stop you from haunting me? I can't stand it anymore."

"Tell the truth. Go to the authorities and tell them you lied in your testimony because you were paid money. And tell them who paid you. Do it immediately. I will be there watching you."

The judge in the case called all the parties into court when he was made aware of the witness who lied. Jean French came in with her head bowed and was told to take the stand. She looked over the room and right in the front row was the stranger who said her name was

Conscience. The room erupted in an uproar when she retracted her testimony and named the high official who had paid her.

The judge looked at her, "are you sure, Madam? If you are, it means you committed perjury in your first testimony. There is a penalty for that."

"Yes," she whispered, "I am sure." She raised her head to look at the stranger but she was gone.

Bethany arrived back home to great applause from Joe.

"I've been following the case," he said, "you're my hero even though I'm the only one who knows that."

"Jean French knows," she said, "but I don't think she'll tell anybody. She wouldn't want people to think she's lost her mind."

"You saved the life of an innocent man and sent a criminal to jail," Joe said. "A hero deserves a hero's reward. Tonight, is yours. I'm taking you to the best restaurant in the city. You can drink all the champagne you want. And later, you can model your negligee for me."

"It sounds like you're planning to take advantage of me," she said.

"I might, my love, I just might," he responded, "with your permission, of course."

END

About the Author

The author has written several books with romance as the topic. Lately he has been exploring the emtional beauty of romance among the stars. This book tells such a story.